The Misfit Hero

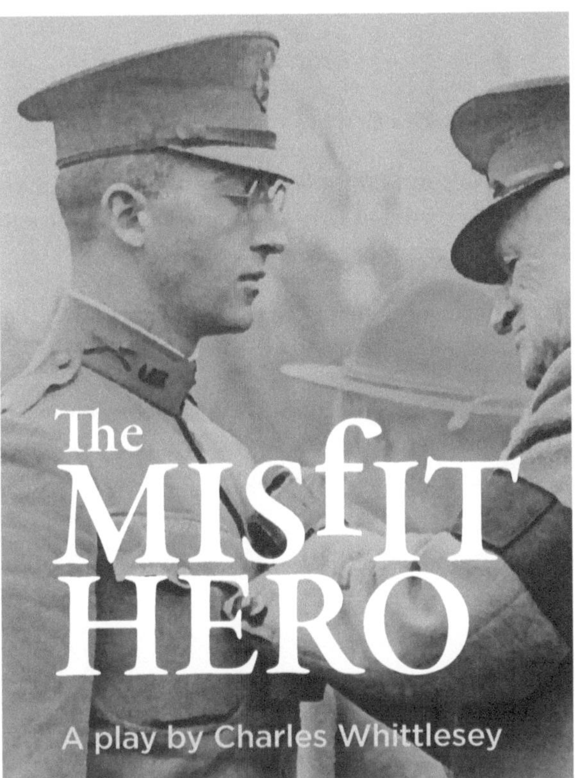
The
MISFIT
HERO
A play by Charles Whittlesey

Applications for performances should be made to Charles Whittlesey at cwhittlesey@charleswhittlesey.com.

Also by Charles E. Whittlesey

Phoebe and Zoe

Summer Solstice: Poems at the Halfway Point in Life

The Islander: A Romance of the Future

The Islander: The Battle for the Future

Cast List

Charles Whittlesey: *a Wall Street Lawyer, age 33*

Marguerite Babcock: *Whittlesey's Girlfriend, age 21*

John Pruyn: *Whittlesey's Law Partner, age 37*

Edith Babcock: *Pruyn's Girlfriend, age 23*

Belvedere Brooks: *a Stockbroker, age 29*

George McMurtry: *a Lawyer, age 41*

Act One

New York City, January 1917

INTERIOR: The Williams Club—Evening

Charles Whittlesey strolls into the Williams Club, newspaper under his arm. He is a tall, lanky man with inquisitive eyes behind a pair of round glasses. He wears a crisp business suit with a pocket watch and chain. He settles into a plush chair and unfolds the paper.

A waiter nears.

WAITER
Evening, Mr. Whittlesey. The usual?

WHITTLESEY
Yes, thank you, Raymond.

The waiter nods and turns away.

WHITTLESEY
Oh, Raymond!

WAITER

(returning)

Sir?

WHITTLESEY
Could I have a cigar as well?

WAITER
What kind?

WHITTLESEY
I don't know. Bring me something ... en vogue.

WAITER
A White Owl?

WHITTLESEY
That will do.

Whittlesey vanishes behind his paper. The waiter returns with a sherry and a cigar and places them on a side table.

WAITER
There you are, sir.
(leaves)

Whittlesey picks up the cigar, lights the tip, inhales, and coughs. He puts down the cigar and takes a sip of sherry. After a pause, he takes another puff, and coughs again, harder. Disgusted, he mashes the cigar into the ashtray.

WHITTLESEY
Serves me right.

Belvedere Brooks strides into the room. Brooks is a tall, athletic man with a confident air. He makes a beeline for Whittlesey.

BROOKS
Charlie! I was hoping I'd catch you here.

WHITTLESEY
(standing)
Bel—what a nice surprise.

They shake hands vigorously.

WHITTLESEY
I haven't seen you in weeks.

BROOKS
I've been as busy as a one-armed paper hanger.

WHITTLESEY
Sit down and tell me about it.

Brooks pulls up a chair and sits.

BROOKS
You don't need me to tell you how bad the markets are.

WHITTLESEY
What's your take on it?

BROOKS
Half the market thinks we're going to war. The other half is worried the war will end. So everybody's selling.

WHITTLESEY
Which camp are you in?

BROOKS
War is coming, Charlie. It's only a matter of time.

WHITTLESEY
I'm not too sure. Most people still oppose it.

BROOKS
That will change when the Germans start sinking our ships.

WHITTLESEY
Oh, come on. They're not that stupid.

BROOKS
They sank the Lusitania.

WHITTLESEY
That was a British ship.

BROOKS
I heard a rumor they're going to sink any ship headed to Europe—that includes American ships.

WHITTLESEY

(frowning)

That would be a foolish mistake.

BROOKS
They'll catch us flat-footed. This country isn't ready for war.

WHITTLESEY
I can't disagree.

BROOKS
(pauses)

We need to prepare. That's why I signed up for officer training camp again.

WHITTLESEY
You did?

BROOKS
Two days ago. In fact, I was hoping you'd join me.

WHITTLESEY
Me? I'm not a soldier.

BROOKS
But you signed up last summer.

WHITTLESEY
That was a four-week course. You're talking about something else—committing to going overseas and fighting.

BROOKS
It's a true test of our ideals. Do we believe in them, or are they just fine-sounding words?

WHITTLESEY
I'm worried for you, Bel. I've read what it's like in the trenches.

BROOKS
I know what I'm getting into. But someone has to do it. And who better than us?

WHITTLESEY

You'll make a first-rate officer. I'm not cracked up for this. You were captain of the Williams football team. I'm just a bookworm.

BROOKS

Don't be so damned modest. You were voted the third-brightest man in our class. You're as disciplined as they come, and you're calmer under pressure than anyone I know. Those are the perfect qualities for an officer—not how many pushups you can do.

WHITTLESEY

That's flattering, Bel, but I can't see myself pointing a gun at my fellow man and pulling the trigger.

BROOKS

They'd put you where you'd do the most good—it might be in a command post or somewhere else behind the lines. No matter where, I know you'd do a first-rate job. We need the best men we have in our officer corps, and you're one of the best men I know. At least say you'll think about it.

WHITTLESEY

I will, but you'll be twice the soldier I could ever be.

BROOKS

You don't know that. A man never knows until he's tested.

WHITTLESEY

It's tempting to know if one can pass the test, but I hope you're wrong, and we never have to face it.

INTERIOR: A Restaurant—Evening

Whittlesey escorts Marguerite Babcock through a restaurant. In her yellow drop-waist dress and hat crowned with red feathers, Babcock turns the heads of the other diners. Whittlesey stops at a table and pulls out a chair.

MARGUERITE
Thank you, Charlie. What a lovely spot.

WHITTLESEY
A lovely spot for a lovely girl.

MARGUERITE

(sitting)

Careful. I might take advantage of your flattery and order something expensive.

WHITTLESEY
I hope you do.

MARGUERITE
That would be like stealing from a child.

WHITTLESEY

(sitting)

Am I such a soft touch?

MARGUERITE
You couldn't hurt a fly, Charlie.

WHITTLESEY

(pensively)

A person doesn't know until he's tested.

MARGUERITE
That sounds ominous.

WHITTLESEY
I spoke with Bel Brooks yesterday. He thinks we're going to war.

MARGUERITE
(coloring)
I don't believe it.

WHITTLESEY
Bel is convinced. He signed up for officer training camp again.

MARGUERITE
Knowing Bel, I'm not surprised. I feel sorry for him.

WHITTLESEY
Why? Bel will make a superb officer. He has all the qualities of a good leader—intelligence, courage, a strong sense of duty.

MARGUERITE
And a single bullet could destroy all those fine qualities.

WHITTLESEY
That's a terrible way to think about it.

MARGUERITE
Does Bel have a magic halo around himself?

WHITTLESEY
Well, I worry about him too. In war, who lives and dies is mostly a matter of chance. Still, I admire him. He believes in what he's doing, and he's willing to risk his life for it.

MARGUERITE
Maybe you should have asked Bel out for dinner.

WHITTLESEY
What does that mean?

MARGUERITE
Nothing.

WHITTLESEY
I think it means something.

MARGUERITE
I know you too well, Charlie. When you admire someone, it's just a matter of time before you think you should do what he is.

WHITTLESEY
Don't you think I have my own principles?

MARGUERITE
You're the most principled man I know, but I always thought your principles lay on the side of pacifism. How many times have you told me this is the most pointless war ever fought?

WHITTLESEY
I still believe that.

MARGUERITE
Thank goodness. For a moment, you had me worried.

WHITTLESEY
But if Bel is right, and they start to sink our ships—with women and children on board—that would be different.

MARGUERITE
I can't believe they would be so cruel.

WHITTLESEY
That's what I told Bel, but he said the Germans are desperate.

MARGUERITE
(picking up her menu)

Do we have to talk about this now?

WHITTLESEY
Of course not. I'm sorry I upset you.

(picks up his own menu)

I'll make it up to you. You were looking for something expensive?

MARGUERITE
Whatever you recommend.

WHITTLESEY
How about the pheasant under glass?

MARGUERITE
It sounds heavenly.

WHITTLESEY
Waiter!

INTERIOR: The Williams Club—Evening

Whittlesey sits in his chair, reading the paper. His body is rigid and his face cross. Finally, he throws down the paper and paces the room.

Bel Brooks enters.

BROOKS
Charlie—have you heard the news!

WHITTLESEY
I just read it.

BROOKS
A cargo ship. Nothing on board but grain. What an outrage!

WHITTLESEY
(putting a hand behind his back)

Well, it was going to Liverpool.

BROOKS
Does it matter? They sank an American ship! That's an act of war!

WHITTLESEY
I wouldn't go to war over a single freighter.

BROOKS
They torpedoed us!

WHITTLESEY
The crew was spared. Did you read the whole article?

BROOKS
Frankly, I was too angry to finish.

WHITTLESEY
The U-boat commander apologized to the captain of the Housatonic. He towed their lifeboats to the nearest British ship. If that was an act of war, it was done in the most gentlemanly way possible.

BROOKS
Gentlemanly? Are you kidding?

WHITTLESEY
No, this was a serious breach of international law, and there must be consequences, but we can't overreact. We have to look at all the facts before we respond.

BROOKS
This is no time to play the lawyer.

WHITTLESEY
I disagree. We have to be cool-headed. If we declare war, there's no going back. Over two million soldiers died last year. On the first day of the Somme, the British lost 20,000 men. Are you willing to trade 20,000 American lives for 3,000 tons of steel?

BROOKS
The German commander clearly had orders to sink the Housatonic. That means they've already set their course. It's going to happen again, and next time, it won't be done in such a gentlemanly way.

WHITTLESEY
Perhaps not, but the right course of action is still diplomacy. We have to convince the Germans that war with us is madness. They can't fight the whole world.

BROOKS
They're counting on us not being ready. It will take us a year to put together an army. By then, the British and French could be finished.

WHITTLESEY
We fought a pointless war in 1812 because our emotions got the best of us. This is not the time to get carried away. Just the opposite. We have to keep our wits and show restraint.

BROOKS
Men may cry, peace, peace—but there is no peace! War is coming, Charlie, and it will be the Germans, not us, who bring it.

WHITTLESEY
I share your outrage, Bel, but if we get baited into this war, we will deeply regret it.

INTERIOR: The Babcock House—Evening

Marguerite and Edith Babcock relax in their parents' drawing room, sipping tea. They are dressed for a night on the town, with their hair curled and faces painted. They are in high spirits, talking fast and laughing often.

MARGUERITE
You'd better be careful. They'll be here any second.

EDITH
We sound like a pair of scheming sisters.

MARGUERITE
Aren't we?

EDITH
We're not scheming. We're speculating.

MARGUERITE
Well?

EDITH
I think Charlie will ask you first.

MARGUERITE
I think John will ask you.

EDITH
They'll have to ask us together. They should know we're a package deal.

MARGUERITE
If one did and not the other, it would be worse than awkward.

EDITH
They wouldn't dare.

MARGUERITE
I'm not so sure. With John, you get what you see. Charlie is different. I feel like there's a part of himself he never shares.

EDITH
Too many books. They make a man indecisive.

MARGUERITE
His mind is the most attractive thing about him.

EDITH
You were always the precocious one.

MARGUERITE
I liked that about him the first time we met.

EDITH
Really? At ten?

MARGUERITE
It wasn't what I saw at first. He was so tall and poised, with such kind, thoughtful eyes. I was quite in awe of him.

EDITH
And he took to you right away.

MARGUERITE
I never could understand why.

EDITH
You reminded him of his poor sister. She would have been your age when she died.

MARGUERITE
I hope I'm more than a substitute.

EDITH

That was 11 years ago. Charlie loves you, I'm sure.

MARGUERITE

I'm sure that he loves me too, but I'm less sure he'll marry me.

EDITH

Applesauce. In a few years, we'll be a happy foursome, with buns in the oven. Think of it, Margot! Won't it be grand?

MARGUERITE

I hope you're right. It's hard to imagine the future any other way.

Muffled voices filter down the hall.

EDITH

Here they are!

John Pruyn and Whittlesey step into the room. Although four years older than Whittlesey, Pruyn, dressed in a tweed cap and checked suit, has an easygoing air that makes him look younger. Whittlesey is dressed more staidly in a dark suit and fedora.

PRUYN

There you are, hiding.

Pruyn sits on the couch beside Edith, takes her hand, and kisses it. Whittlesey sits across from Marguerite. He smiles and winks at her.

EDITH

(rubbing Pruyn's hand)

It must be cold out.

PRUYN

Bitterly.

EDITH
You need some hot tea.

PRUYN
Splendid idea.

EDITH
Charlie?

WHITTLESEY
Yes, thank you.

Edith pours tea for Pruyn and Whittlesey.

WHITTLESEY
Are you sure you want to go out in this cold?

EDITH
You'll have to keep us warm.

PRUYN
Wouldn't miss the chance, would we, Charlie?

WHITTLESEY
Never. Especially as you both look so lovely tonight.

MARGUERITE
(blushing)

Thank you, Charlie.

PRUYN
I think we'd be warmer if we fortified the tea.

He reaches into his jacket and pulls out a flask.

PRUYN
Edith?

EDITH

Careful. If mother and father see you, they'll never let you back.

PRUYN

They're reading in the den.

Edith puts a finger to her lip, holds out her cup, and grins. Smiling, Pruyn gives her a splash.

PRUYN

Charlie?

Charlie holds out his cup.

PRUYN

Margot?

MARGUERITE

I don't want to spoil the party.

Pruyn pours in a few drops.

WHITTLESEY

A toast to our little quartet. May we always make beautiful music together.

They toast and sip their tea.

INTERIOR: Pruyn & Whittlesey Law Office—Afternoon

Whittlesey sits at his desk, writing a letter. There is a knock on the door, and Belvedere Brooks walks in, followed by a husky middle-aged man with a rugged face that clashes with his pressed suit.

WHITTLESEY

(standing)

Bel, what brings you here?

BROOKS

I'm sorry to bother you at work, Charlie, but this couldn't wait.

WHITTLESEY

You look out of sorts.

BROOKS

Something dire has occurred. Do you know George McMurtry?

WHITTLESEY

I know the name.

MCMURTRY

(shaking Whittlesey's hand.)

Pleased to meet you, Mr. Whittlesey.

WHITTLESEY

You fought with Teddy Roosevelt at San Juan Hill.

MCMURTRY

I did a lot of foolish things when I was young.

WHITTLESEY
Or brave things.

MCMURTRY
There's a fine line between the brave and the foolish. I was lucky enough to live through it. That's what matters.

BROOKS
George just told me something important.

WHITTLESEY
(Motions his guests to chairs. They all sit.)

Let me guess, Bel—still recruiting?

BROOKS
Once you hear this, I won't need to.

WHITTLESEY
What happened? There's nothing in the papers.

BROOKS
It's not in the papers yet.

MCMURTRY
I have a good friend in the state department. The news he passed along is strictly confidential.

WHITTLESEY
You can count on my discretion.

MCMURTRY
Bel said as much.

WHITTLESEY
Has there been another sinking?

MCMURTRY
Worse. The British got hold of a German telegram to Mexico. The Huns not only said they're going to sink our ships, but they asked Mexico to join them. In return, they promised to hand over Arizona, New Mexico, and Texas!

WHITTLESEY
(stunned)
That's appalling.

MCMURTRY
When this gets in the papers, President Wilson will have no choice but to declare war.

WHITTLESEY
What did Mexico say?

BROOKS
It doesn't matter, Charlie. Germany has essentially declared war on us.

MCMURTRY
You're right, Charlie. Bel and I are recruiting. We're calling on a few handpicked men we believe would make first-rate officers, and Bel says you have all the desired qualities. We'll need good men in this war. It will test our country like nothing ever has.

WHITTLESEY
(stands and paces behind his desk)
You were right, Bel.

BROOKS
What do you say, Charlie? Can we count on you?

WHITTLESEY
Are you reenlisting, George?

MCMURTRY
I already have. They don't have chains strong enough to hold me back.

WHITTLESEY

(thinking)

I'm not one for on-the-spot decisions, but I believe this calls for a vigorous response.

BROOKS
There's only one response possible.

MCMURTRY
It's no small decision, Mr. Whittlesey. Please consider it carefully. But remember your country is waiting for your answer.

INTERIOR: A Restaurant—Evening

Whittlesey sits across from Marguerite in a fine restaurant. He stares at the menu while tapping his fingers on the table.

MARGUERITE
You seem nervous tonight, Charlie.

WHITTLESEY
Do I? Well, I have a lot on my mind.

MARGUERITE
Is this a special occasion?

WHITTLESEY
Well, it is an occasion.

MARGUERITE
You're acting funny. I wish you'd relax.

WHITTLESEY
I wanted to speak with you about something important.

MARGUERITE

(expectantly)

Yes?

WHITTLESEY
I'm enlisting.

MARGUERITE

(stunned)

What?

WHITTLESEY
I signed up for officer training camp. After that, I'm not sure where I'll go.

MARGUERITE
But just a few weeks ago you said—

WHITTLESEY
I know what I said, but I just learned some disturbing news. I can't tell you what, but I can tell you with absolute certainty that we're going to war.

MARGUERITE
How can you know that?

WHITTLESEY
You'll hear about it soon. When the news comes out, the whole country will be up in arms.

MARGUERITE
I can't believe that you, of all people, would enlist.

WHITTLESEY
Do I seem so unpatriotic?

MARGUERITE
How many times have you told me this war had nothing to do with us?

WHITTLESEY
That changed when they started sinking our ships.

MARGUERITE
Has there been another one?

WHITTLESEY
No, but there will be, and soon.

MARGUERITE
I don't believe it.

WHITTLESEY
Nobody wants to believe it, but it's true.

MARGUERITE
But why are you enlisting? You can't even shoot a quail. Now you're going to shoot people?

WHITTLESEY
Well, that's what a soldier does.

MARGUERITE
For God's sake, you're a socialist.

WHITTLESEY
Can't a socialist defend his country?

MARGUERITE

(touching her forehead)

I'm so confused.

WHITTLESEY
I can't stay here, dining in fine restaurants, while my countrymen bear all the hardship.

MARGUERITE
What about your practice?

WHITTLESEY
John will take care of it. We've already worked out the details.

MARGUERITE

(pauses, then tears up)

And what about me?

WHITTLESEY
I know it must be a shock.

MARGUERITE

A shock? You brought me to this beautiful place. I got all dressed up, expecting ... and instead you tell me the worst possible news!

WHITTLESEY

(blushing)

I didn't realize—

MARGUERITE

Please don't embarrass me any further.

She stands up and throws her napkin on the table.

WHITTLESEY

You're not leaving?

MARGUERITE

I am.

WHITTLESEY

Please, Margot. This isn't easy for me either.

MARGUERITE

It's easier than sticking to your principles. That would call for some real courage—standing up to your friends no matter what they said. You think you're being brave, don't you, running off to war, when the really brave thing would be to say no, I'm not participating in this perversion of patriotism. The truth is, you're not a patriot, you're a coward. I thought you were a better man, Charles Whittlesey, but I can see I was wrong.

She turns and storms out. Whittlesey glances around, red-faced, and then dashes after her.

Act Two

Argonne Forest, October 1918

EXTERIOR: Argonne Forest—Night

Fog envelops the stage. Coils of barbed wire loom in the mist. Beyond the wire, bushes choke the landscape. Overhead, artillery shells whistle, coming more and more rapidly. They land in the distance, flashing in the dark and rumbling the earth. As the barrage intensifies, the sound and light overwhelm the senses.

Lines of doughboys march down the aisles and spread out before the stage. When the shelling stops, Major Charles Whittlesey climbs a ladder onto the stage, turns, and faces his men.

WHITTLESEY

The time of trial is here. Beyond that wire lies the Hun. This is the final push, the beginning of the end, and the shortest way home is over that wire and straight through Germany.

I know that some of you are new to this. I won't lie to you. You will see things you've never seen before, or wish to see again, and they will frighten the bravest among you. Remember that being scared isn't the measure of a man. The measure of a man is what he does even when he's scared. I know you're all good men, lion-hearted and strong. We will do our part for our country, come what may.

The rest of you know what lies ahead. Give the Germans hell. They'll be sure to give it back. Help the new men if you can. The recruit whose life you save today could save yours tomorrow.

Follow your orders and stick to the plan. Remember your spacing. If you stick together, you'll make easy targets.

Sergeant, ready the men. Men, steel yourselves. I know all of you will do your duty. Your duty to your country. To your family back at home. To the man standing beside you. We will push ahead as one man, with one will and one goal—victory!

He takes a pair of long-handled wire cutters from the sergeant, clamps a whistle between his lips, and draws his service revolver. The shriek of the whistle pierces the night.

WHITTLESEY

Let's go!

(he rushes forward)

The men climb the ladders, lumber into the fog, and disappear. After a pause, the chugging of machine guns breaks the stillness.

EXTERIOR: Argonne Forest—Twilight

Whittlesey and Lieutenant Cullen huddle among the bushes. Behind them, a group of soldiers crouches and waits. In the clearing ahead, a footbridge crosses a stream.

WHITTLESEY

(pointing)

Our objective is that hill. We'll cross the stream in single file, fan out, and dig in on the near slope.

LIEUTENANT CULLEN

(scratching his head)

I don't like the looks of that.

WHITTLESEY

Why not?

LIEUTENANT CULLEN

The hills are crawling with Huns. If we cross that bridge, we'll be cut off.

WHITTLESEY

That's always a possibility, Lieutenant Cullen.

LIEUTENANT CULLEN

I'd say it's more of a certainty.

WHITTLESEY

You know our orders. We are to reach our objective regardless of flanks or losses.

LIEUTENANT CULLEN

If we cross that bridge, we'll be trapped. They'll murder us.

WHITTLESEY
I'm more worried about the German artillery. The slope of that hill will protect us.

LIEUTENANT CULLEN
Not from the rear.

WHITTLESEY
We'll set up runner posts back to our lines.

LIEUTENANT CULLEN
It won't matter. We're too far forward.

WHITTLESEY
Are you suggesting we disobey orders?

LIEUTENANT CULLEN
Can't we dig in here? We're just a little bit shy.

WHITTLESEY
In a ravine?

LIEUTENANT CULLEN
We could back up a ways.

WHITTLESEY
We are not going backward. How many men did we lose to get here? We're not going to pay for the same ground twice.

LIEUTENANT CULLEN
If we get surrounded, how many men will we lose?

WHITTLESEY
Did you know I've been told to shoot any man who disobeys an order?

LIEUTENANT CULLEN
You can't really mean that, sir.

WHITTLESEY

Of course not. But orders are orders. General Alexander is depending on us to reach that hill. I'm not going to second guess him. Sometimes orders have a purpose we can't see from the ground.

LIEUTENANT CULLEN

And sometimes we can see things from the ground the generals can't.

WHITTLESEY

(sharply)

That's enough, Lieutenant. Get your men moving.

LIEUTENANT CULLEN

(grumbling)

Yes, sir.

Cullen waves his men over the bridge. They hurry across and vanish among the trees.

EXTERIOR: Argonne Forest—Morning

In a dugout covered by a fallen tree, Majors Whittlesey and McMurtry talk in low voices. Around them, soldiers crouch in their fox holes. Sporadic shells land nearby. A soldier hurries through the brush and jumps into the dugout.

WHITTLESEY
What did you find?

PRIVATE
The runner lines are gone, sir.

MCMURTRY
What do you mean, gone?

PRIVATE
The fox holes are still there, but no sign of our boys.

MCMURTRY
How far back did you go?

PRIVATE
Two posts. I couldn't get no further. I heard voices ahead'a me—German voices.

WHITTLESEY

(exchanges looks with McMurtry)

Did you actually see them?

PRIVATE
I can't see ten feet in this woods, but I heard what I heard. And that ravine we came through last night is fulla barbed wire now.

WHITTLESEY
All right, private. Report back to your post.

PRIVATE
(cautiously)

Sir, are we surrounded?

WHITTLESEY
The Huns are always trying to sneak behind us. Don't worry, we'll teach them a lesson.

PRIVATE
(smiling)

Yes, sir. We'll give 'em hell.

WHITTLESEY
That's the spirit.

The private climbs out and hurries away.

WHITTLESEY
Any sign of the French yet?

MCMURTRY
No. Our left flank is wide open.

WHITTLESEY
And the right?

MCMURTRY
No sign of the 307th. We seem to be alone.

An artillery shell lands close by with a deafening boom.

WHITTLESEY
If the Germans get our range, we'll be in trouble. You'd better find Teichmoeller.

MCMURTRY
Good idea.

(climbs out of the dugout)

Whittlesey unfolds a map and studies it. McMurtry returns with Lieutenant Teichmoeller.

LIEUTENANT TEICHMOELLER
Yes, sir.

WHITTLESEY
That trench mortar is getting our range. We need some counter fire.

LIEUTENANT TEICHMOELLER
I'll send a runner back.

WHITTLESEY
The runner lines are down. You'll have to send a pigeon.

LIEUTENANT TEICHMOELLER
I'll find Private Richards.

WHITTLESEY
It's coming from the northwest. Do you need coordinates?

LIEUTENANT TEICHMOELLER
I'll work them out, sir. We'll drop a load of hell right on top of 'em.

WHITTLESEY
Excellent.

Lieutenant Teichmoeller salutes and leaves the dugout.

MCMURTRY
I think by now we have to assume the Germans are behind us.

WHITTLESEY
The question is, where? And how many?

MCMURTRY
There's only one way to find out.

WHITTLESEY
We'll test the line. Let's send Holderman and Company K to the left and Wilhelm with Company E to the right.

MCMURTRY
They're both good men. They'll get the job done.

WHITTLESEY
Soon we'll know exactly where we stand.

On stage right, Lieutenant Teichmoeller gives a note to Private Richards, who folds it into a small aluminum capsule. Richards takes a pigeon out of a cage, ties the capsule to a foot, and throws the pigeon into the air.

PRIVATE RICHARDS
Fly home, my friend! Fly home!

EXTERIOR: Argonne Forest—Day

Whittlesey crouches in the command post, writing a message. His chin is stubbled, and his shirt is speckled with blood and caked with dirt. His face is drawn but intensely focused. Rifle and machine-gun fire crackle, and the occasional mortar shell lands close by. In the distance, pigeons coo nervously.

WHITTLESEY

(writing and reading aloud)

Germans are still around us ... We have been heavily shelled by mortar this morning. Present effective strength ... total here about 235. Officers wounded: Lieutenant Harrington, Captain Stromee, Lieutenants Peabody and Revnes. Lieutenant Wilhelm, Company E, missing. Cover bad if we advance up the hill and very difficult to move the wounded if we change positions. Situation is cutting into our strength rapidly. Men are suffering from hunger and exposure, and the wounded are in very bad condition. Cannot support be sent at once?

McMurtry enters, limping. His left knee is bandaged and blood-stained.

MCMURTRY

Cullen sent the Huns packing. God, that man knows how to fight.

WHITTLESEY

Casualties?

MCMURTRY

No reports yet, but not many, I think.

WHITTLESEY

We can't afford many.

MCMURTRY
They'll hit us again this afternoon, like clockwork.

WHITTLESEY
What's that?

In the distance, artillery shells thunder. The sound gradually moves closer.

MCMURTRY
They must have gotten our pigeon.

(pointing to the balcony)

It's moving up those hills.

The barrage lands in the German lines. The Germans scream and the Americans cheer.

MCMURTRY
Now the Huns are getting theirs.

WHITTLESEY
Those sound like 155s.

MCMURTRY
I'm damn glad they're ours.

The artillery grows louder.

WHITTLESEY
I don't like the sound of that.

MCMURTRY
It's moving down the hill!

WHITTLESEY
It had damn well better stop.

MCMURTRY
It's still coming!

WHITTLESEY

(jumps to his feet)

Everybody down! Take cover!

The barrage hits the American lines and settles in. Moans rise up as men are hit. Whittlesey dashes recklessly among the fox holes.

WHITTLESEY
Take it easy! This can't last long. They'll realize their mistake any time now. Stay calm!

The shelling continues, now a deafening roar. Men scream as they die. Whittlesey runs back to the dugout. A trickle of blood flows down his nose. He shouts at McMurtry.

WHITTLESEY
Get me Private Richards!

McMurtry rushes out. Whittlesey squats and scribbles out a note.

WHITTLESEY

(writing and reading aloud)

To the commanding officer, 308th Infantry. We are along the road parallel 276.4. Our own artillery is dropping a barrage directly on us. For heaven's sake, stop it.

Private Richards enters the dugout with a crate on his back. Inside, two pigeons coo frantically.

PRIVATE RICHARDS
Major, are you okay?

WHITTLESEY

(Looks up, frowns, and removes a piece of shrapnel under his glasses. He stares at it for a second and then throws it aside.)

This is our only hope. Send it right away.

Richards stuffs the note into a capsule and pulls a pigeon out of the cage. A shell lands nearby, startling him, and the bird flies away. He lunges for it, but misses.

WHITTLESEY
Fuck!

PRIVATE RICHARDS
I'm sorry, sir!

He reaches into the cage and grabs the last pigeon.

PRIVATE RICHARDS
Come on, Cher Ami. It's up to you now.

He clips the capsule to Cher Ami's foot and throws him skyward. The Americans crane their necks as the pigeon circles and lands in a tree. They groan in despair.

WHITTLESEY
Can't you do something?

PRIVATE RICHARDS
(picks up a stick and throws it at the bird)
Hey! Cher Ami! Get outta here!

Whittlesey and the others join in, shouting and throwing sticks at the pigeon. Cher Ami doesn't budge. Finally, Richards bounds over to the tree, climbs it briskly, and shakes the branches.

PRIVATE RICHARDS
Come on you goddamn bird! Fly!

Cher Ami lifts off, circles twice, and flies away. A shell lands directly below it, dropping her from the sky.

PRIVATE RICHARDS
No!

WHITTLESEY
Get me another pigeon!

PRIVATE RICHARDS
There ain't no more, sir.

WHITTLESEY
Then get one of Tollefson's.

PRIVATE RICHARDS
Teddy's gone, sir. All his birds too.

MCMURTRY
If we move to the left, I think we can escape the worst of it.

WHITTLESEY
The German artillery can hit us there.

MCMURTRY
We can move back when our own guns stop.

WHITTLESEY

(thinking)

All right. Put the word out. Move everyone 50 yards to the left. Then come and help me with the wounded.

EXTERIOR: A Pigeon Loft—Day

A bell rings. A soldier enters and finds a blood-stained pigeon in the coop. He reaches in and gently removes it.

PIGEON HANDLER

What happened to you, poor fella?

(examines the bird)

Right in the chest ... one eye, one leg.

(carefully unties the capsule)

Hanging by a thread.

(opens the tube and reads the message)

God forgive us!

(stuffs Cher Ami back in the cage and runs offstage)

Major! Quick! Stop the shelling! Stop the shelling!

EXTERIOR: The Infirmary—Day

Whittlesey enters the infirmary, a hollow in the ground. The medics are struggling to move the wounded, who moan and cry out in pain. To one side, a pile of bodies forms a wall. Whittlesey stares at it in horror.

MEDIC
Sir?

Whittlesey doesn't answer.

MEDIC
Major?

WHITTLESEY
(composing himself)

Yes?

MEDIC
We can't move some of these men. They won't make it.

WHITTLESEY
If they stay here, they won't make it either.

MEDIC
I guess not.

WHITTLESEY
And cover up these men.

MEDIC
(stares at the wall)

With what?

WHITTLESEY
Dirt, branches. Whatever you can find.

MEDIC
We'll do our best.

The shelling stops abruptly. An eerie calm spreads over the pocket.

WHITTLESEY
Cher Ami. Incredible.

MEDIC
Thank God. Can we keep the men here?

WHITTLESEY
Of course.

McMurtry rushes into the infirmary.

MCMURTRY
The Huns are forming up again!

WHITTLESEY
Where?

MCMURTRY
Left, right, center.

WHITTLESEY
Let's shore up our lines. Come on!

They hurry off as machine guns rake the pocket.

EXTERIOR: Argonne Forest—Night

Whittlesey sits on a log in the dugout. A beam of moonlight pierces the leaves overhead and lights up his drawn face. He pulls a letter from his pack, unfolds it slowly, and holds it up to the light.

BROOKS
Dear Charlie, I only have time for a quick note. We're heading back to the front again. I think the big push is coming. God willing, it will go as planned, and we'll be home by Christmas.

My heart soared when I heard they gave you command of the battalion. I know you'll make an outstanding commander. At the same time, it made me nervous to know you'd be leaving the command post and coming directly to the front, where you'll be more exposed. I know you too well, Charlie. You're not one to lead from behind, and you would never make your men take risks you wouldn't take yourself. But I beg you not to be a hero. Not only for my sake, but for the sake of your men. They would be sure to suffer without your steady hand.

Let us hope that luck stays with us both, my brother, and we'll have many occasions to sit together at the Williams Club and look back on these hard days as the most noble and virtuous of our lives. I wish you Godspeed, Charlie. May the angels protect you and guide you swiftly and safely on the shortest path home.

Your dear friend,
Bel

Whittlesey cries.

MCMURTRY

(stirring from his sleep)

You all right?

WHITTLESEY

(straightening and wiping his tears)

I'm fine.

MCMURTRY
Is that from your girl?

WHITTLESEY
It's from Bel.

MCMURTRY
Ah.

WHITTLESEY

(stashing away the letter)

I don't know why I keep it.

MCMURTRY
I'm sure his wife would like to read it.

WHITTLESEY
I suppose.

MCMURTRY
Did you ever find out what happened?

WHITTLESEY

(nods)

They were being shelled. He stopped to let his men inside a cave. They made it. He didn't.

MCMURTRY
Then he died a hero.

WHITTLESEY
He told me not to play the hero, but he couldn't take his own advice.

MCMURTRY
When we signed up, we all knew we might not come home.

WHITTLESEY
I'm beginning to think we're not getting out of here, George.

MCMURTRY
You can't let the men know that.

WHITTLESEY
I think the men know it too.

MCMURTRY
As long as we hold on, so will they.

WHITTLESEY
I'm damn proud of them, aren't you?

MCMURTRY

(nodding)

Four days with no food or water. Sleeping in the mud and their own shit. Shot to hell with nothing but rags to bind their wounds. Still, they keep fighting.

WHITTLESEY
I always thought my friends back home were so impressive, but they're nothing compared to these men. Most don't have a dime to their names. Some of them can't even speak English, let alone read it. Still, I've never served with finer men.

MCMURTRY

All that matters now is grit. Our boys have it in spades.

WHITTLESEY

You had it backwards, George. It's the men who inspire me, not the other way around. As long as they hold on, so will I.

MCMURTRY

If we keep our nerve, we'll be all right. If we start doubting ourselves, we're finished.

WHITTLESEY

Don't worry. Whether or not our boys find us in time, our course will be the same.

MCMURTRY

I'm glad to hear you say it. Now get some rest. They'll hit us again when the sun comes up.

EXTERIOR: Argonne Forest—Day

Whittlesey and McMurtry sit in the dugout, staring into space. A bloody bandage covers McMurtry's shoulder. Sporadic gunfire crackles around them.

Private Hollingshead enters and salutes.

MCMURTRY

(stands)

Holly! We thought you were dead.

PRIVATE HOLLINGSHEAD

I did too, sir.

WHITTLESEY

(stands and approaches him angrily)

Private Hollingshead, why did you leave your post?

PRIVATE HOLLINGSHEAD

I'm sorry, sir. We were starving to death. We tried to find the food our planes dropped.

WHITTLESEY

How many went with you, and where are they now?

PRIVATE HOLLINGSHEAD

Nine, sir. The ones in front were killed. The rest of us were taken prisoner.

WHITTLESEY

You escaped?

PRIVATE HOLLINGSHEAD
No, sir. Lieutenant Prinz let me go.

WHITTLESEY
Lieutenant Prinz?

PRIVATE HOLLINGSHEAD
The German commander. Gosh, he spoke better English than me. They treated me like a king. They fed me! A whole plate of roast beef and a loaf of bread. Their bunker was big as a mansion!

WHITTLESEY

(darkly)

What did you tell him?

PRIVATE HOLLINGSHEAD

(blushing)

Nothing, sir. I swear.

WHITTLESEY
Then how do you find yourself back here?

PRIVATE HOLLINGSHEAD
The lieutenant said to give you this.

(reaches into this pocket, pulls out a letter, and hands it over)

WHITTLESEY

(reads the letter out loud)

To the Commanding Officer of the Second Battalion ... Sir. The bearer of the present, Private Lowell R. Hollingshead has been taken prisoner by us ... He has been charged against his will ... in carrying forward this present letter to the officer in charge ... to recommend to this commander to surrender with his forces, as it would be quite useless to resist any more in view of the present conditions. The suffering of your wounded men can be heard over here in the German lines and we are appealing to your humane sentiments. A white flag shown by one of your men will tell us that you agree with these conditions ... The German commanding officer.

Whittlesey and McMurtry look at each other.

PRIVATE HOLLINGSHEAD
What do you think, sir?

WHITTLESEY
Are the white panels for our planes still up?

MCMURTRY
They are.

WHITTLESEY
Take them down right away.

PRIVATE HOLLINGSHEAD
Does that mean we're not surrendering?

WHITTLESEY

(angrily)

Private Hollingshead, you had no business leaving your post without direct orders from your officer—which you did *not* have. You put the entire regiment in danger.

PRIVATE HOLLINGSHEAD

(coloring)

I'm sorry, sir.

WHITTLESEY

Go back to your post, immediately. And if you say one word about the roast beef, I'll have you court-martialed.

PRIVATE HOLLINGSHEAD

Yes, sir.

He salutes, turns, and hurries away.

MCMURTRY

Do you think he told them anything?

WHITTLESEY

I don't think he needed to. They can see for themselves.

MCMURTRY

May I?

Whittlesey hands him the letter. McMurtry reads it and looks up, smiling.

MCMURTRY

They wouldn't send this if they weren't slipping. We've got 'em licked.

WHITTLESEY

Don't be too sure. They'll give us one last push with everything they have.

MCMURTRY

I wonder how the men will take it.

In the distance, shouting breaks out.

PRIVATE 1
Rot in hell, you Heinie son of a bitch!

PRIVATE 2
Come and get us, you Kraut bastards!

PRIVATE 3
Come on down, you Bosch bastard! I'll cut off your balls and stuff 'em down your throat.

WHITTLESEY
They sound ready.

MCMURTRY
Let the Huns come. We'll make them wish they hadn't.

EXTERIOR: Argonne Forest—Dusk

Whittlesey and McMurtry stand in the dugout, talking in low voices.

MCMURTRY
They chased the Huns down the road, howling like demons. Scared the hell out of'em.

WHITTLESEY
They scared the hell out of me too.

MCMURTRY
They're sleeping on the ground where they stopped.

WHITTLESEY
I don't think they can do it again. We're out of ammunition. One more attack and we're finished.

SOLDIER
(entering the dugout)

Sir, there's a captain on the road who wants to see you.

MCMURTRY
A captain?

WHITTLESEY
Stay here, George. I'll see what it's about.

Whittlesey leaves the dugout. A handful of doughboys emerge from the woods, pinching their noses and gagging.

LIEUTENANT TILLMAN
Major Whittlesey?

WHITTLESEY
Who the devil are you?

LIEUTENANT TILLMAN
Lieutenant Tillman, 307th. We're relieving you. We have food on the way.

WHITTLESEY
You are a most welcome sight, Lieutenant. How did you find us?

SOLDIER
We followed the smell.

MCMURTRY
(catches up with Whittlesey and claps him on the back)
Relieved, Charlie! Can you believe it?

WHITTLESEY
I can't.

MCMURTRY
God has found us fit to spare.

WHITTLESEY
And all these men. Thank Him for that.

LIEUTENANT TILLMAN
(reaches into his bag and takes out a sandwich)
You look hungry.

Whittlesey grabs the sandwich and tears into it.

MCMURTRY
For God's sake. Give me some of that.

TILLMAN
I have another.
(hands a sandwich to McMurtry)

WHITTLESEY
Do you have any water?

SOLDIER
Take mine.

(offers him a canteen)

Whittlesey and McMurtry pass the canteen back and forth and grin at each other as they inhale their sandwiches.

Act Three

New York City, November 1918

EXTERIOR: New York Dockyards—Day

A freighter rests against a dock in New York Harbor. Marguerite Babcock, John Pruyn, and Edith Babcock stand nearby.

MARGUERITE
There he is!

Whittlesey, dressed in civilian clothes, strides down the gangplank.

PRUYN

(waving)

Charlie!

Marguerite runs forward and hugs him.

MARGUERITE
I'm so happy to see you!

WHITTLESEY
And I, you.

MARGUERITE
Thank God you're all in one piece.

PRUYN

(shaking Whittlesey's hand)

Welcome home, Charlie.

EDITH

(hugging Whittlesey)

We were so worried. The news was awful.

WHITTLESEY
The news?

PRUYN
Didn't you know? The papers have been writing about you. The whole country knows about the Lost Battalion.

WHITTLESEY
The Lost Battalion?

EDITH
That's what they're calling it. Everybody's talking about you, Charlie. You're a hero.

WHITTLESEY
(taken aback)
Me?

PRUYN
We heard about the surrender note. When you told the Germans to "go to hell."

WHITTLESEY
I said no such thing.

PRUYN
Well, frankly, it didn't sound like you.

A group of reporters enters.

REPORTER 1
Look—it's Go-to-Hell Whittlesey!

They rush up to Whittlesey, crowding back his friends.

REPORTER 1
How does it feel to be home, Major?

WHITTLESEY
Who are you?

REPORTER 1
John Hanks, New York Tribune.

WHITTLESEY
Surely, the Tribune has more important things to write about.

REPORTER 1
No, sir. Right now, you're the biggest story in the country.

WHITTLESEY
You can't be serious.

REPORTER 2
You don't think the Lost Battalion is important?

WHITTLESEY
The men who fought in it are important. And by the way, we were never lost. The Germans knew exactly where we were.

REPORTER 2
(writing frantically)

That's more like it!

REPORTER 3
Where are your men now?

WHITTLESEY
In La Chalade, getting some well-earned rest.

REPORTER 1
Is it true you got promoted?

WHITTLESEY
Yes, to Lieutenant Colonel.

REPORTER 2
When do you get your medal?

WHITTLESEY
What medal?

REPORTER 2
The medal of honor.

WHITTLESEY

(blushing)

I hope you're wrong about that.

REPORTER 2
No, sir. We have official word from the U.S. Army.

WHITTLESEY

(shaking his head)

The men are the ones who deserve medals. There are so many who did more than I.

REPORTER 3
Just how bad did it get over there?

WHITTLESEY
No matter how bad it got, the boys never wavered. If you want stories, you should write about them.

REPORTER 3
They won't be back for months.

WHITTLESEY
I'm sorry, gentlemen, please excuse me. I wasn't ready for this, and my friends are waiting.

He jostles his way through the reporters. Marguerite and Edith each take an arm, and they hurry offstage pursued by reporters, shouting questions.

EXTERIOR: Central Park—Day

Whittlesey and Marguerite walk arm-in-arm down a bridle path. Whittlesey is wrapped in a long winter coat. Marguerite wears a fur-collared coat and cloche hat. The grass is brown and the trees are bare, but the sky is a brilliant blue.

WHITTLESEY
It's calming here, Margot. Thank you for braving the cold.

MARGUERITE
We should do this more often. It would take your mind off things.

WHITTLESEY
Lately, that's been getting harder.

MARGUERITE
Are you already tired of being a hero?

WHITTLESEY
I never wanted to be one.

MARGUERITE
Your men will be home any day now. That should take the spotlight off you.

WHITTLESEY
There's going to be a parade. The whole regiment is supposed to march down Fifth Avenue.

MARGUERITE
How grand. Aren't you excited?

WHITTLESEY

They want me to lead it—riding a horse! Can you imagine that? What a fool I'll look, prancing around like General Custer.

MARGUERITE

You'll have to put aside your modesty for a day.

WHITTLESEY

If it were only a day. Every time I visit my parents, there's a mob of reporters waiting there. I have to fight my way in, and then they run around the house and peek through the windows.

MARGUERITE

I never knew that fame could be so troublesome.

WHITTLESEY

They always ask me to read that damn surrender note—as if I kept it in my pocket—and shout, "Go to hell!"

MARGUERITE

Maybe you should tell them to go to hell.

WHITTLESEY

I'd love to. They're more stubborn than the Germans.

MARGUERITE

Sooner or later, they'll latch onto some other story. Then you can think about your future, instead of your past.

WHITTLESEY

(guiltily)

I know what you're saying. There are things we should have discussed by now.

MARGUERITE

I'm just happy you're home, Charlie. I can't imagine what you went through. Nobody expects you to walk off a boat and act like nothing happened.

WHITTLESEY

Some people can, apparently.

MARGUERITE

A brute, maybe. I wouldn't want to be connected with such a person.

WHITTLESEY

You have a kind way of putting it.

MARGUERITE

Sort yourself out. Find the old Charlie. Then we can talk about other things.

WHITTLESEY

You're a saint, Margot.

(lets out a hollow cough)

MARGUERITE

I don't like the sound of that.

WHITTLESEY

It's the cold air.

MARGUERITE

We should have stayed inside.

WHITTLESEY

Don't worry. I'm fine.

MARGUERITE

Have you seen a doctor?

WHITTLESEY

(shaking his head)

I know what he'd say—rest, eat right, exercise.

MARGUERITE

(stops)

Charles Whittlesey—promise me this minute you'll see a doctor before the week is over.

WHITTLESEY

All right. If only to keep you happy.

MARGUERITE

I'll hold you to that. Now let's go inside. I won't be known as the woman who killed the commander of the Lost Battalion.

INTERIOR: Pruyn Law Office—Day

Whittlesey sits at his desk behind stacks of books, writing. His pen dries up. He dabs the tip into an inkwell, but the pen only scratches the paper. He picks up another pen and dips it in, but it too leaves no mark. He stares at the pen and frowns.

A knock startles him. In the doorway stands a young man on crutches. His right leg is missing.

WHITTLESEY

(stands and smiles)

There's a familiar face.

KURTZ

(smiling broadly)

Good to see you again, sir.

WHITTLESEY

None of that sir business. It's Mr. Whittlesey—better yet, Charlie.

(walks around, shakes Kurtz's hand, and pulls out a chair)

Have a seat.

KURTZ

(leans his crutches against the desk and slowly sinks into the chair)

Thank you, sir. This is quite a place.

WHITTLESEY

(sits)

Forgive me, it's Private Kurtz, right?

KURTZ

Yes sir. Tom Kurtz.

WHITTLESEY
Company H, with Lieutenant Cullen?

KURTZ
I think we had the worst of it.

WHITTLESEY
I knew we could always count on you. I hope you're damn proud of yourself.

KURTZ
You're very kind, sir.

WHITTLESEY
How are you getting along?

KURTZ
Frankly, not so good. Gangrene took my leg.

WHITTLESEY
I'm sorry.

KURTZ
I shouldn't complain. I was lucky to get back. So many guys didn't.

WHITTLESEY
Are you working now?

KURTZ
Not much. Nobody wants to hire a cripple.

WHITTLESEY
What's your line of work?

KURTZ
I'm a bricklayer.

WHITTLESEY
Surely you can still lay bricks.

KURTZ
That's what I keep telling 'em, but they don't want to hear it. They think I'm damaged goods.

WHITTLESEY
Nonsense. You can do more with one leg than most men can with two. Can I write you a recommendation?

KURTZ
That would be a great honor, sir. Do you know of any jobs? I'd take just about anything.

WHITTLESEY
Not at the moment, but if I do, I'll be sure to let you know.

KURTZ
I need to find something soon. My rent is two months overdue. They said they'd throw me on the street.

WHITTLESEY
How much is your rent?

KURTZ
Fifteen dollars.

WHITTLESEY
(takes out his wallet)

That should take care of it.

KURTZ
Thirty dollars! Thank you, sir!

WHITTLESEY
Spend it all on rent, Tom.

KURTZ
What else would I do with it?

WHITTLESEY
You smell like a distillery.

KURTZ
(clears his throat)

It calms me down. I still have nightmares. Terrible nightmares.

WHITTLESEY
Drinking will only make them worse.

KURTZ
Don't you worry, sir, I'll use it right. God bless you. You were the best officer we ever had.

WHITTLESEY
And you were the bravest men I ever knew.

Choking up, Kurtz stands and salutes.

WHITTLESEY
Come back tomorrow and I'll have that letter.

KURTZ
Thank you, sir. I can't say it enough.

(salutes and leaves)

Whittlesey stares at the floor, stands, and paces. Pruyn enters.

PRUYN
Everything all right, Charlie?

WHITTLESEY
No, everything is not all right.

PRUYN
What's the matter?

WHITTLESEY
Every day this week someone from my old regiment has come by.

PRUYN
I'm sorry. We'll do a better job of screening them.

WHITTLESEY
It wouldn't be right to turn them away.

PRUYN
I guess not. Times are hard right now.

WHITTLESEY
(steps to the window and looks down)
Take a look outside.

PRUYN
(goes to the window)
What am I looking for?

WHITTLESEY
How many reporters do you see?

PRUYN
None.

WHITTLESEY
Those two men on the corner—they've been here all morning.

PRUYN
Wait—that fellow in the porkpie hat tried barging in yesterday.

WHITTLESEY
And the man across the street, stuffing a hot dog into his face. That makes four.

PRUYN

Reporters or hot dogs?

WHITTLESEY

I'm glad you're keeping your sense of humor, but there's no reason to put up with this. I shall have to submit my resignation.

PRUYN

Resignation? Have you lost your marbles?

WHITTLESEY

I can't get a thing done. Worse, I'm disrupting the whole office. You can't afford to pay us for doing nothing.

PRUYN

You're mistaken. We've gotten more business because of you.

WHITTLESEY

If that's what's bringing in business, I want none of it. Last week, Case & White made me an offer. I told them no, but now I've changed my mind. It's a big firm, and I can blend in without causing any trouble.

PRUYN

Charlie, we've been partners for eight years. This practice was our dream.

WHITTLESEY

And now it's becoming a nightmare.

PRUYN

(staring hard at Whittlesey)

You really mean it, don't you?

WHITTLESEY
I don't see any other way.

PRUYN
What am I supposed to do without you?

WHITTLESEY
Live your dream, John. You can easily run the practice without me. You're a newlywed. Enjoy your wife.

PRUYN
If I let you go, Edith will be upset with me.

WHITTLESEY
She has a right to be upset with me, but not you.

PRUYN
Does Marguerite know?

WHITTLESEY
Please don't tell her. I'll do it myself.

PRUYN
Are you sure you know what you're doing?

WHITTLESEY
The more I think about it, the more sure I am. I'm sorry, John, but consider this my official notice. I'll wrap up my cases and leave by the end of the month. Trust me, it will be better for both of us.

INTERIOR: The Babcock House—Afternoon

Edith and Marguerite sit in their parents' drawing room. Edith, six months pregnant, is crocheting a blanket while Marguerite reads Women in Love.

EDITH
How was your date with Charlie?

MARGUERITE
(looking up)
I'm not sure it was a date.

EDITH
Then what was it?

MARGUERITE
A confabulation.

EDITH
Is that all?

MARGUERITE
Sometimes I wonder if he really loves me.

EDITH
How can you doubt it?

MARGUERITE
I don't understand, Edith. When he sees me, he beams. He takes me out to dinner. He laughs at my jokes. I can see it in his eyes—there's tenderness, affection, and pleasure in my company. But I've known him ten years, and he's barely even kissed me.

EDITH

(tilting her head)

Have you ever wondered if he's funny?

MARGUERITE
Funny in the head?

EDITH
No. Funny.

MARGUERITE
I don't know what you mean.

EDITH
Maybe he doesn't like women.

MARGUERITE
Applesauce. He puts women on pedestals.

EDITH
Don't be a Dumb Dora. You know what I'm saying.

MARGUERITE
Edith!

EDITH
It never crossed your mind?

MARGUERITE
Charlie is a war hero, a successful lawyer. He's—

EDITH
A confirmed bachelor.

MARGUERITE
Lots of men are confirmed bachelors.

EDITH
And lots of confirmed bachelors are funny.

MARGUERITE
If you weren't my sister, I'd slap you.

EDITH
Don't get cross with me. You know I love Charlie.

MARGUERITE
I'm not so sure now.

EDITH
A finer man never walked the earth. I couldn't care less whom or what he liked, but I love my sister too, and I'm starting to worry she's chasing a man she's never going to catch.

MARGUERITE

(hurt)

You just said he loved me.

EDITH
I love you, too. That doesn't mean I want to bear your children.

MARGUERITE
Since he came home he hasn't been the same. The war changed him.

EDITH
That could be it too.

MARGUERITE
Whenever I ask him about it, a curtain drops. I always regret bringing it up.

EDITH
Maybe you should take the bull by the horns.

MARGUERITE
How would I do that?

EDITH
Ask him. Do you love me? Are you going to marry me?

MARGUERITE
A lady doesn't ask a man that kind of thing.

EDITH
No, but a lady should be clever enough to learn the answer without having to ask. Of course, it's different if she doesn't want to know.

MARGUERITE
You think I'm fooling myself.

EDITH
Honestly, I don't know, but I think you need to find out soon. You're almost 24. You'll never be prettier than you are now.

MARGUERITE
As if that was all that mattered.

EDITH
Like it or not, it matters.

MARGUERITE

(pouting)

You've ruined my whole day.

EDITH
Better than ruining your whole life.

MARGUERITE
That hurts.

EDITH

I'm sorry to pain you, sister, but the sooner you find out, the better.

(sets down her needles and stands)

I'm off to the bathroom again. It's a mother's curse.

Edith leaves. Marguerite walks to the window and looks out glumly.

MARGUERITE

Oh, Charlie. What on earth are you doing?

INTERIOR: Case & White Law Office—Day

Whittlesey sits at his desk, working intently on his papers. His secretary appears in the doorway.

SECRETARY
I'm sorry to bother you.

WHITTLESEY
(looks up, exasperated)
Not again.

SECRETARY
It's a Mrs. Geller.

WHITTLESEY
Oh.

SECRETARY
She said that her—

WHITTLESEY
Yes, yes, I know.

SECRETARY
What should I say?

WHITTLESEY
(rubbing his forehead)
You'd better send her in.

The secretary leaves. Whittlesey stands and paces. A short, heavy woman stops in the doorway and stares at him nervously.

WHITTLESEY

(approaching)

Mrs. Geller? It's good to meet you.

(he guides her to a chair)

MRS. GELLER

You know me?

WHITTLESEY

I knew your son, of course.

MRS. GELLER

I was afraid you wouldn't remember him.

WHITTLESEY

I remember them all.

MRS. GELLER

They say you're a good man, Mr. Whittlesey.

WHITTLESEY

What can I do for you?

MRS. GELLER

I wanted to ask you about Hyman.

WHITTLESEY

Of course you do. I'm so sorry, Mrs. Geller.

MRS. GELLER

What kind of a soldier was Hyman?

WHITTLESEY
He was a fine soldier. He carried out his orders without question. The other men liked him. He was not only a good soldier, but a good man, a brave man. I was lucky to have the honor of commanding him.

MRS. GELLER
(sniffles)

That's my Hyman.

WHITTLESEY
You have everything to be proud of, Mrs. Geller. I am so sorry I couldn't bring him home to you.

MRS. GELLER
How did he go?

WHITTLESEY
Pardon?

MRS. GELLER
How did he die?

On stage right, Private Geller, screams in pain as he writhes in a pool of his own blood. Both of his legs are missing. Mrs. Geller freezes. Whittlesey gets up from his desk, walks slowly over to Private Geller, squats, and takes his hands.

MEDIC
(rushing in)

Good God.

WHITTLESEY
(waving the medic away)

It's all right. You're going to be all right.

PRIVATE GELLER
I can't feel my legs!

WHITTLESEY
You caught a bit of shrapnel. The medic is here. He'll patch you right up.

PRIVATE GELLER
I don't want to die!

WHITTLESEY
You're not going to die.

PRIVATE GELLER
Mother! Mother! Mother!

Geller's body goes limp. Whittlesey stays with him, holding his hands. Finally, he pries away his fingers, walks back to his desk, and sits. He stares at his hands, covered in blood.

WHITTLESEY
A bullet through the heart. Instant. He felt no pain.

MRS. GELLER
(crying)
Did you bury him?

MEDIC
(rolls Geller onto a stretcher)
Soldier—gimme a hand.

SOLDIER
Where to?

MEDIC
The infirmary.

SOLDIER
Why? He's dead.

MEDIC
We need him in the wall.

WHITTLESEY
We buried him where he fell. One of the men said a few words. Given the situation, it was the best we could do.

MRS. GELLER

(still crying)

Forgive me. I know it's not easy for you, but a mother needs to know these things. Knowing my son did his duty, that he didn't suffer much, it helps, you know, it helps make the burden lighter.

WHITTLESEY
I'm glad I could reassure you. If there's any other way I can help, let me know.

MRS. GELLER

(rises from her chair)

They were right. You are a good man. I'm glad Hyman served with you.

WHITTLESEY
The honor was mine, Mrs. Geller, all mine.

She walks away slowly. Whittlesey watches her leave, goes to the window, and cries.

EXTERIOR: Streets of New York—Night

Huddled in his winter coat, Whittlesey prowls the streets on a cold, foggy night. On the rooftops, pigeons coo mournfully. A church bell chimes twice, then stops. A man emerges from the fog. Whittlesey freezes.

WHITTLESEY
What the devil?

BROOKS
Hello, Charlie.

WHITTLESEY
Bel?

BROOKS
I didn't mean to startle you.

WHITTLESEY
Startle? You harrow me with fear and wonder.

BROOKS
Are you the melancholy prince of Denmark?

WHITTLESEY
More like mad King Lear.

BROOKS
It's me, Charlie. Trust your eyes.

WHITTLESEY
What about my mind?

BROOKS
Your mind is sound. It's your heart I worry about.

WHITTLESEY
Some days it weighs a thousand pounds.

BROOKS
That rests hard on my conscience. It wasn't my place to push you.

WHITTLESEY
I made my own choice. So did you.

BROOKS
You know it's not that simple.

WHITTLESEY
(stares at Bel intently)

You know, don't you?

BROOKS
Of course.

WHITTLESEY
Did you love me too, Bel?

BROOKS
I loved you, Charlie, like a brother.

WHITTLESEY
There's a knife through the heart.

BROOKS
I'm sorry. The last thing I want is to hurt you.

WHITTLESEY
(drops his head)

I'm a misfit, Bel. I have always been and will always be.

BROOKS
What did you hope to gain?

WHITTLESEY
Your respect? Your admiration?

BROOKS
You always had both.

WHITTLESEY
But I might have lost them.

BROOKS
We knew each other too well for that.

WHITTLESEY

(struggling)

Is it uncommon to want to share the hardships of someone you love?

BROOKS
It's just like you to see it that way.

WHITTLESEY

(puts his head in his hands)

I'm so ashamed.

BROOKS
You have nothing to be ashamed of, Charlie, nothing.

WHITTLESEY
Don't I? I'm a fraud at everything—as a patriot, as a hero, and as a man.

BROOKS
I hate to say it, Charlie, but you're one of the most rigid human beings I ever knew. You have this unbending ideal of what a man should be, and you refuse to change even if it kills you.

WHITTLESEY
They wouldn't be ideals if we ignored them when inconvenient. You had the same ideals yourself.

BROOKS
And they destroyed me. You need to change yours, Charlie, before they destroy you.

WHITTLESEY

(shaking his head)

Honestly, I wouldn't know where to start.

BROOKS
Start with the girl. She has a right to know the truth.

WHITTLESEY
I think she already knows.

BROOKS
Then why hold on to her?

WHITTLESEY
I do love her, you know.

BROOKS
Not the way that she loves you.

WHITTLESEY

(drops his head)

I know it's unfair.

BROOKS
It's unfair to you as well. Sometimes you need to uproot the past before you can plant the future.

WHITTLESEY
If only I knew what to plant.

BROOKS
Start with the truth. We can figure out the rest later.

WHITTLESEY
Does that mean I'll see you again?

BROOKS
I've never left your side.

WHITTLESEY
(moved)
I've always felt you there.

BROOKS
Keep the faith, Charlie. We'll meet again.
(turns into the fog and disappears.)

WHITTLESEY
(stepping forward)
Bel?

The church bell rings twice. Whittlesey looks around nervously and then strides away.

EXTERIOR: Central Park—Afternoon

Whittlesey and Marguerite walk arm in arm through the park. The leaves are burnt yellow and fiery orange, but the grass is still green. Whittlesey looks tired and distant. Marguerite's red coat and feathered hat belie the tension on her face. Whittlesey coughs harshly.

MARGUERITE
Your cough sounds worse.

WHITTLESEY
It comes and goes.

MARGUERITE
You promised to see a doctor.

WHITTLESEY
I did see one.

MARGUERITE

(stops and lets go of his arm)

What did he say?

WHITTLESEY
Nothing helpful.

MARGUERITE
Charlie—for Heavens' sake—tell me.

WHITTLESEY

(starts walking again)

Right before the big push, our command post got hit by a shell. It contained phosgene gas.

MARGUERITE
Phosgene?

WHITTLESEY
It smells like freshly cut hay. Not unpleasant, really, but if you breathe much in, you suffocate. I was lucky. All I have is the cough.

MARGUERITE
All this time and you never told me?

WHITTLESEY
I was hoping it would go away.

MARGUERITE
It's worse, not better.

WHITTLESEY
Some days I'm fine and some days I'm not. I don't know why.

MARGUERITE
It's worse when you're upset.

WHITTLESEY
Is it?

MARGUERITE
Whenever you visit the Red Cross or see one of your men.

WHITTLESEY
Those are moral obligations. I can't say no.

MARGUERITE
I heard you accepted command of your regiment again.

WHITTLESEY
The regiment is decommissioned. It's only a title.

MARGUERITE

(bitterly)

Edith said you're giving away money to your men. She said there's a regular line at your door, and you never turn them down.

WHITTLESEY

I can't, Margot.

MARGUERITE

Doesn't there have to be a limit to your giving?

WHITTLESEY

You don't understand war.

MARGUERITE

I hope I never do.

WHITTLESEY

In a battle, you have to order a man to charge across a field into a hail of bullets. He knows he could be crippled or killed, but he does it anyway—without hesitation or complaint. And if you're the one giving him that order, and he follows it, how can you deny him the one small favor he asks of you?

MARGUERITE

(emotionally)

You're right, I don't understand war, but I do understand what's happening to you, Charlie, and I'm frightened.

WHITTLESEY

Hush now.

MARGUERITE

You can't go on like this. You have to do something.

WHITTLESEY
What more could I possibly do?

MARGUERITE
Go somewhere they'll leave you alone. Where the air is dry and your lungs can heal. Why not California? I could go with you, Charlie. We could start a new life together.

WHITTLESEY

(stops)

California?

MARGUERITE
Yes, Charlie. For God's sake, let's go.

WHITTLESEY
I can't see it working.

MARGUERITE
Why not?

WHITTLESEY
I can't leave my family. My parents are old, and they need my help. My brother Elisha is sick. This is where my life is. I belong here.

MARGUERITE

(angrily)

At least you could tell me the truth.

WHITTLESEY
I don't know what you mean.

MARGUERITE
You won't go because you don't love me.

WHITTLESEY
That's not true. I won't go because I do love you.

MARGUERITE
I don't believe you.

WHITTLESEY
I'm an albatross around your neck.

MARGUERITE
Nonsense.

WHITTLESEY
You deserve a happy life with a normal, healthy man, not a life spent nursing a cripple.

MARGUERITE

(crying)

You're not a cripple, Charlie. The truth is, you're too strong for your own good.

WHITTLESEY
If I were strong, I would have set you free years ago.

MARGUERITE
I don't want to be free.

WHITTLESEY
You'd be happier.

MARGUERITE

(wiping away her tears)

I was always partial to albatrosses.

WHITTLESEY

(smiling)

Even when they wear spectacles?

MARGUERITE

(laughing)

You see, we do belong together.

WHITTLESEY

We're good together, Margot, but that doesn't mean we'd be happy together.

MARGUERITE

Don't say no out of hand. Think about it, will you? That's all I'm asking.

WHITTLESEY

All right, Margot. You're right about one thing. We can't go on as we have. Either I have to change or we do.

INTERIOR: Case & White Law Office—Day

Whittlesey stands by his office window, brooding. There is a knock on the door and George McMurtry steps in. He is bright-eyed and brimming with energy, wearing a striped suit.

WHITTLESEY
George!

MCMURTRY
(striding over to Whittlesey)
Charlie!

They shake hands vigorously. Their faces flush with emotion.

WHITTLESEY
You look well, George. Damn well.

MCMURTRY
It's good to see you, Charlie. How are you?

WHITTLESEY
I'm doing fine.

MCMURTRY
You look tired. Up to your old tricks? Working too much?

WHITTLESEY
Old habits die hard. What brings you here, George?

MCMURTRY
Didn't you get the letter?

WHITTLESEY
You wouldn't believe how much mail I get.

MCMURTRY
There's going to be a dedication at the Tomb of the Unknown Soldier. We've been chosen as honorary pallbearers. It's next Friday.

WHITTLESEY

(blanches)

Friday?

MCMURTRY
President Harding is giving the address. Most of Congress will be there, the Supreme Court too. It will be a day for the history books. What's wrong? I thought you'd be excited.

WHITTLESEY

(goes behind his desk and sits)

Far from it.

MCMURTRY

(pulls out a chair, sits, and studies Whittlesey)

What's wrong, Charlie?

WHITTLESEY
I don't want to burden you.

MCMURTRY
Dammit, after all we've been through? What's the matter?

WHITTLESEY

(sighs)

Not a day passes without someone in our old outfit coming by, usually about some sorrow or misfortune. I wish they would leave me alone.

(pauses)

I cannot bear much more.

MCMURTRY
I had to fight my way through a mob of reporters in your lobby. I assumed they were here because of the letter.

WHITTLESEY
They are here every day.

MCMURTRY
No wonder you're tired.

WHITTLESEY
I don't suppose I could turn it down?

MCMURTRY
You can't mean that.

WHITTLESEY
I do. Frankly, I don't want to go.

MCMURTRY
You're still in command of the regiment, Charlie. It's an order.

WHITTLESEY
I suppose it is.

MCMURTRY
Maybe it would help put things behind you. One last rite to close out the past.

WHITTLESEY
I've been trying to close that door a long time, but people keep pushing it open.

MCMURTRY
You need a holiday.

WHITTLESEY
I have been thinking about a trip.

MCMURTRY
We could meet in Atlantic City the day after. Have you ever been?

WHITTLESEY
No.

MCMURTRY
You'd love it. Seven miles of boardwalk overlooking the sea. Hotels as big as Buckingham Palace. Music, parades, rides. They turn a blind eye to hooch, and other things too.

WHITTLESEY
It would be nice to have a beer again.

MCMURTRY
It would do you a world of good. What do you say?

WHITTLESEY

(thinks for a minute)

All right, George. It would be good to spend some time with you again.

MCMURTRY
We need to keep in better touch. Call me anytime, day or night.

WHITTLESEY
We'll have a grand time in Atlantic City. I'll keep my mind on that.

INTERIOR: Whittlesey's Bedroom—Night

Whittlesey lies in bed, twitching in his sleep. His movements grow more violent. Finally, he bolts upright and screams. Just as suddenly, he stops screaming and freezes.

On the other side of the wall, a fist pounds.

MUFFLED VOICE
Shut the hell up in there!

Whittlesey coughs uncontrollably.

MUFFLED VOICE
Stuff a sock in it! You're drivin' me crazy!

With great effort, Whittlesey stifles his cough. He gets up, dresses quickly, and throws on a coat. He leaves his boarding house and walks through the dark, foggy streets of Manhattan. As he nears a street lamp, a figure emerges from the fog and stops him cold.

WHITTLESEY
Bel.

BROOKS
You seem less glad to see me now.

WHITTLESEY
If I needed any more proof I'm going mad, you are surely it.

BROOKS
Why didn't you tell her, Charlie?

WHITTLESEY
I lost my nerve. I couldn't tell her I wasted so many years of her life.

BROOKS
All the more reason to.

WHITTLESEY
She knows it's time to move on, even if she doesn't know why.

BROOKS
I'm not so sure you made that clear.

WHITTLESEY
I thought it was crystal clear.

BROOKS
To you, maybe.

WHITTLESEY
Did you come just to reproach me?

BROOKS
What would she think about your latest plan?

WHITTLESEY

(stares hard at Brooks, then looks away)

What plan is that?

BROOKS
You can't hide it from me.

WHITTLESEY

(grumbling)

Apparently not.

BROOKS
Why Cuba?

WHITTLESEY
Does it matter?

BROOKS
It doesn't.

WHITTLESEY
I've thought it through carefully. I've weighed all the pros and cons. There is no easy way out, no magic key. Every move I make ends in checkmate.

BROOKS
What about your parents and your brothers?

WHITTLESEY
It will be easier on everyone, even if they don't understand.

BROOKS
You can predict the future now?

WHITTLESEY
No, but I can plot the mark of an arrow by its path.

BROOKS
The future isn't a straight line. It's a branch. Every fork is a choice, and every choice alters your path. No one knows the end until he reaches it.

WHITTLESEY
I'm sorry, Bel. I could have made different choices before, but not now. There are no more forks left in this branch.

BROOKS
Maybe there's a fork you refuse to consider.

WHITTLESEY

I know what you're suggesting. Give up my responsibilities to the regiment? How can I? How can I abandon the men whose lives I destroyed? How can I disgrace the honor of the men who died? If they gave up their lives, who am I to cast off my burdens and run away?

BROOKS

I don't know, Charlie, maybe none of us can really change. But we can stay open to new possibilities. Keep your eyes open for another branch. If you have your eyes fixed on a certain path, you won't see any other way, and that would be a terrible loss.

WHITTLESEY

(thinking)

I'll keep my eyes open, Bel, but changing my course now would take a miracle.

BROOKS

Miracles do happen. God be with you, Charlie. And so will I, no matter what.

He steps back into the fog and disappears.

EXTERIOR: Boardwalk in Atlantic City—Day

Whittlesey and McMurtry stroll along a crowded Boardwalk. A soft breeze comes off the ocean, and a gentle surf laps the beach. The sun is shining. Whittlesey is dressed casually in a sport coat. McMurtry wears a checked jacket and a boater hat. Now and then, someone in the crowd stops and stares at the two men, trying to remember them, but then moves on.

MCMURTRY
Put your money in bonds, Charlie. The slump is over. The markets are going gangbusters.

WHITTLESEY
That's worked out very well for you.

MCMURTRY
A fool could make money in this market. But you have to play the game.

WHITTLESEY
I was never very good at games.

MCMURTRY
You're too serious. That's why I thought this place would do you good. Do you like it?

WHITTLESEY
It does calm the mind.

MCMURTRY

(sighing)

What a splendid view. Did you ever think we'd get to enjoy a day like this again?

WHITTLESEY
Truthfully, the minute I landed in France, I assumed I was dead.

MCMURTRY

And you should've been, the way you strode around the pocket. Luck's a funny thing. We left so many behind, and yet here we are, just because a shell landed in one place and not the other.

WHITTLESEY

It doesn't make sense. Why should they have died and we have lived?

MCMURTRY

Why should we have died and they have lived? You can't change what luck chose for you, but you can enjoy the gift you were given.

WHITTLESEY

Your view is much healthier than mine. I envy how you seem to shrug it off.

MCMURTRY

(grudgingly)

I wouldn't say that. I have nightmares too.

WHITTLESEY

How do you deal with them?

MCMURTRY

I get up and go to work.

WHITTLESEY

That's it?

MCMURTRY

(shrugs)

Sometimes I talk to Mabel.

WHITTLESEY

Surely, she can't understand.

MCMURTRY
No, and I leave out as much as I say, but it's nice to have someone listen and let you know you're not crazy. You can't bottle yourself up. If you don't find a way to let off the steam, you'll explode.

WHITTLESEY
I've done a poor job of that.

MCMURTRY
How did it go yesterday?

WHITTLESEY
I kept thinking it was one of our men in that casket.

MCMURTRY
Highly unlikely.

WHITTLESEY
I know, but I couldn't shake the feeling.

MCMURTRY
How do you feel today?

WHITTLESEY
Surprisingly, I feel a strange sense of relief.

MCMURTRY
Good. Sooner or later, people will forget about the war and get on with their lives. Then you can get on with yours. It will all fade with time. You just have to wait it out.

WHITTLESEY
You're so down-to-earth, George. It cheers me up to see you. I can't tell you how much I value our friendship.

MCMURTRY

(patting Whittlesey on the back)

The same goes for me. Now what do you say we have that beer?

WHITTLESEY

As you said, maybe it's time to blow off a little steam.

INTERIOR: A New York Bistro— Night

Whittlesey and Marguerite sit at a corner table. Whittlesey eats his spaghetti, seemingly at ease, while Marguerite twirls her pasta nervously.

MARGUERITE
Are we going somewhere after dinner?

WHITTLESEY
I didn't make any plans. What do you feel like doing?

MARGUERITE
Maybe a play? A comedy?

WHITTLESEY
I doubt we could get tickets.

MARGUERITE
They'll find us seats, I guarantee it.

WHITTLESEY
Then we'd be taking the seats of two other people.

MARGUERITE
What if we could choose the people? We could choose two people who deserved to be drowned.

WHITTLESEY

(chuckles)

You're wicked tonight, Margot.

MARGUERITE

(turning grave)

I'm afraid I am.

WHITTLESEY
You almost sound serious.

MARGUERITE
I am serious.

WHITTLESEY
(sets down his fork)
What's wrong?

MARGUERITE
I've been meaning to tell you for a long time.

WHITTLESEY
Better late than never.

MARGUERITE
(pauses)
I've been dating someone.

WHITTLESEY
Dating?

MARGUERITE
Oh, come on, Charlie. You can't be surprised.
You've been home for ages.

Whittlesey shrugs.

MARGUERITE
I'm not a young girl anymore. I can't wait—

WHITTLESEY
There's no need to explain. It makes perfect sense.

MARGUERITE
It does?

WHITTLESEY
My life is much too complicated. I can't control it anymore.

MARGUERITE

(bitterly)

Or you refuse to.

WHITTLESEY
I can't change who I am.

MARGUERITE
I can see that now.

WHITTLESEY
You'll be better off without me.

MARGUERITE
You might not be.

WHITTLESEY
Never mind about me. Is he a good man?

MARGUERITE
He's a fine man.

WHITTLESEY
He treats you well—gives you everything you deserve?

MARGUERITE
More than I deserve.

WHITTLESEY
Then I'm happy for you.

MARGUERITE
At least you could give me the pleasure of being jealous.

WHITTLESEY
I am jealous. You'll make him a very happy man.

MARGUERITE
I want a family, Charlie.

WHITTLESEY
Of course you do. No need to say anything more. Let's finish our dinner and go see a play. We'll find the two loudest boors in the audience and toss them into the street. We'll make a gay night of it.

MARGUERITE
I would love that, Charlie.

WHITTLESEY
This is a night to celebrate.

(lifts his glass)

To you, Margot, and to all the happiness you so justly deserve.

MARGUERITE

(lifts her glass)

To you, Charlie, and to all the happiness that you deserve.

INTERIOR: Bar in the S.S. Toloa—Night

Whittlesey sits at a table, nursing a beer. Across him sits a man in a linen suit and Panama hat, sipping a daiquiri.

WHITTLESEY
The strange thing is, the Kaiser, the Czar, and King George were cousins.

MR. MALORET
You don't say?

WHITTLESEY
Their grandmother was Queen Victoria.

MR. MALORET
Are you suggesting the Great War was nothing but a family feud?

WHITTLESEY
I'm not suggesting it, I'm asserting it.

MR. MALORET
(shakes his head)

Twenty million dead because of three jealous cousins.

WHITTLESEY
And we let ourselves get sucked into the maelstrom.

MR. MALORET
I don't mean to presume, Mr. Whittlesey, but that must leave a bitter taste after everything you and your men went through.

WHITTLESEY
You're Puerto Rican, Mr. Maloret. I can speak frankly with you. If I said this back at home, they'd hang me for treason. They blame everything on the Germans.

MR. MALORET
It seems to me they do bear most of the blame.

WHITTLESEY
Perhaps, but there's plenty to go around.

MR. MALORET
Honestly, I don't know how you could have stayed neutral. I'm an exporter. I knew people who went down on your ships.

WHITTLESEY
When they sank the Lusitania, I was horrified. But now I wonder. You've heard the rumor she was carrying arms.

MR. MALORET
It's my business to know such things. The hold was packed with ammunition.

WHITTLESEY
We were kidding ourselves by claiming to be neutral. The Germans knew better.

MR. MALORET
That's quite a statement, coming from a decorated war hero.

WHITTLESEY
A medal doesn't change the truth.

MR. MALORET
I suppose not.

WHITTLESEY
In my case, I made a choice. I have no one else to blame. The men who served under me were drafted. They were forced to serve.

MR. MALORET
How true. It's refreshing to hear an American be so frank.

WHITTLESEY
It's one thing to talk about it over a beer, years later. It's another thing to hold the hands of a dying boy with his legs blown off. That's a sight you can never forget.

MR. MALORET

(frowning)

The world isn't what it should be. Full of such horrors, but such beauty too.

(sighs)

At least we're safe and warm here, on our way to a paradise. I think Cuba will be good for you. People there know how to live.

WHITTLESEY
I'm looking forward to the change.

MR. MALORET
I raise my glass to you, Mr. Whittlesey—for your gallant service to your country and for a better life ahead.

The two men raise their glasses and drink.

WHITTLESEY

(sets down his glass)

Thank you, Mr. Maloret. I've enjoyed our conversation, but the hour is late, and it's high time I retired.

He stands abruptly and walks out the bar.

EXTERIOR: Deck of the S.S. Toloa—Night

Whittlesey steps onto the empty deck. Overhead, the stars glimmer, but in the distance, clouds boil up and blot them out. In their billowy heights, thunder peals. Whittlesey goes to the railing and looks down. A wave of fog curls over the deck. He turns and faces the audience.

WHITTLESEY

No matter where I go, this wretched fog pursues me. That day I charged into it, I should have been the first man killed. Better to have died before the pocket, before the false glory, the nightmares, and the guilt. The last three years of my life have been pointless. Even better for mother and father to welcome home a flag-draped coffin than to witness the sad, slow spectacle of my undoing.

Forgive me, mother, for the pain I've caused you—and for the pain I've yet to cause. You brought me into the world, raised me with love, shaped my character, and forgave my flaws, but now you are helpless to heal my wounds.

(looks up at the stars)

When I was young, you told me the stars were our lost loved ones, staring down at us and smiling. Russel. Frank Jr. Annie. But when I look at them now, all I see are the flickering lights of my own men. Mother, dear, mother, how many new stars have I added to the skies?

> They stare down at me, asking me *Why?* Why did I have to die? And I have no answer to give them.
>
> I hear your voices calling me. I know each of your names, your faces, and the way you died. I no longer have a place among the living, and now I belong with you, the dead. In truth, I have been dead for years and have only been marking time before I could join you. At last, the hour has come to leave behind this world of darkness and fog and find my peace in the bright, comforting lights of our eternal brotherhood.

He straddles the rail, reaches into his jacket, and pulls out his service revolver. The fog slowly envelops him. The foghorn lets out a deep, resonant blast, and when a gust of wind sweeps the fog away, Whittlesey is gone.

EXTERIOR: Pittsfield Cemetery—Morning

Marguerite stands in front of the Whittlesey family monument, holding a bouquet. Etched in the stone are the names of Frank R. Whittlesey, Jr., Annie E. Whittlesey, Russell Whittlesey, and Charles White Whittlesey. Marguerite approaches a footstone and stares down.

MARGUERITE

(smiling weakly)

Hello, Charlie. I know you'd laugh at me for doing this—but it comforts me to think you can hear me, so your laughter won't stop me. Besides, I finally have a captive audience, and I know you'd laugh at that too.

I never dreamed we'd end up here. I had such a different vision of our lives. When we first met, I thought I had found my soul mate. And you treated me like an equal, not just a girl.

You opened up my life to so many things. You taught me to love this world's beauty and to cherish fine words and deeds. Our walks in the woods, the poems you quoted so easily, and the clever stories you told—they all left their mark on me. You brought out the best in me and suppressed everything that was petty or vain.

A man like you is a rare thing in this world. I knew that even as a young girl. I had quite a crush on you, Charlie, from the very start.

But I hung on too long. I should have known it wasn't meant to be. And after the war, you couldn't belong to anyone except your men. I hope that God has healed both their wounds and yours. Maybe it's better that you're together now, in a world unblemished by ugliness and hate.

(crouches and sets the bouquet on Whittlesey's grave)

God bless you, Charlie. If any soul deserves the words Rest in Peace, it's you.

She kisses her fingertips and places them gently on the bouquet.

Epilogue

In 1922, Whittlesey's brother Elisha died from complications of phosgene gas poisoning. Whittlesey's only remaining sibling, Melzar, had one son who died at the battle of Guadalcanal in World War II.

In 1925, John Pruyn and Edith Babcock divorced.

Cher Ami received the Croix de Guerre with a Palm and Oak Leaf Cluster. After her death, she was mounted and displayed in the Smithsonian Institute.

In 1938, the Survivors of the Lost Battalion held its first reunion. George McMurtry footed the bill for the yearly gatherings until his death in 1958. His estate covered the costs until the final meeting in 1968.

In 1922, Marguerite Babcock married Francis J. Sinnott, a decorated war veteran. He was a postmaster, a county clerk, and a leader of the Brooklyn Democratic Party. They raised four children together. Marguerite died in 1989 at the age of 93.

www.ingramcontent.com/pod-product-compliance
Ingram Content Group UK Ltd.
Pitfield, Milton Keynes, MK11 3LW, UK
UKHW041640190726
13854UKWH00006B/2610

9 798493 928598